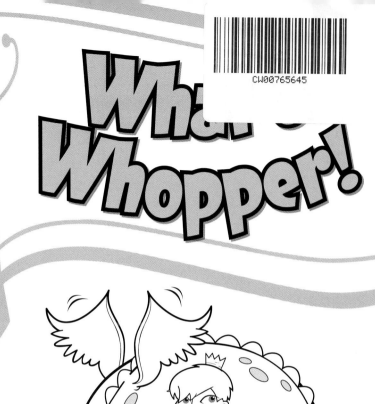

What a Whopper!

Written by Jill McDougall
Illustrated by Ash Oswald

Published by Pearson Education Limited, 80 Strand, London, WC2R 0RL.

www.pearsonschools.co.uk

First published in 2012 by Pearson Australia.
This edition of *What a Whopper!* is published by Pearson Education Limited by
arrangement with Pearson Australia. All rights reserved.

Text © Pearson Australia 2012
Text by Jill McDougall

Original illustrations © Pearson Australia 2012
Illustrated by Ash Oswald

22 21 20 19 18
10 9 8 7 6 5 4 3 2 1

British Library Cataloguing in Publication Data
A catalogue record for this book is available from the British Library

ISBN 978 0 435 19451 2

Printed in China by Golden Cup

Acknowledgements
We would like to thank the following schools for their invaluable help in the
development and trialling of the Bug Club resources: Bishop Road Primary
School, Bristol; Blackhorse Primary School, Bristol; Hollingwood Primary School,
West Yorkshire; Kingswood Parks Primary, Hull; Langdale CE Primary School,
Ambleside; Pickering Infant School, Pickering; The Royal School, Wolverhampton;
St Thomas More's Catholic Primary School, Hampshire; West Park Primary School,
Wolverhampton.

Note from the publisher
Pearson has robust editorial processes, including answer and fact checks, to ensure
the accuracy of the content in this publication, and every effort is made to ensure
this publication is free of errors. We are, however, only human, and occasionally
errors do occur. Pearson is not liable for any misunderstandings that arise as a
result of errors in this publication, but it is our priority to ensure that the content
is accurate. If you spot an error, please do contact us at resourcescorrections@
pearson.com so we can make sure it is corrected.

CONTENTS

Chapter 1 Reggie's Birthday 4

Chapter 2 Flicker 10

Chapter 3 Sir Plants-a-Lot 13

Chapter 4 Where's Flicker? 19

Chapter 5 Upper Twaddle 25

Chapter 6 Hayfields 31

Chapter 7 Reggie Saves the Day 35

Reggie's Birthday

Near the town of Upper Twaddle, there was a tatty old castle. In the castle lived a king, a queen and their son Reggie. The king and queen were poor. In fact, they had no money at all.

Every day, and twice on Fridays, the king sang funky pop songs outside the castle gate. People threw stale bread and turnips into his crown. Then they hurried away with their fingers jammed in their ears.

The queen worked hard in the royal cabbage patch, picking slugs off the cabbages. She planned to sell the cabbages at the Royal Fair.

Prince Reggie hung out in his bedroom playing with his Tower Power Building Set.

Two days before the Royal Fair, something amazing happened. Reggie had his eighth birthday. (This was not the amazing thing.)

The king gave Reggie an extra large turnip wrapped in purple string. (This was not the amazing thing either.) The queen gave Reggie a slug to keep as a pet. Was this the amazing thing?

Nooo.

The amazing thing happened after supper. First, there came a timid knock at the castle door.

Rat-a-tat.

Reggie swung the door open.

CREEEEAK!

There, sitting on the steps, was the amazing thing.

"Whoopee!" cried Reggie. "A real birthday present."

There was a little box, and on top of it was a message:

Happy Birthday Reggie!
From Great-Aunt Lulu
P.S. Handle with EXTRA care.

Reggie gasped. What could it be?
A football? Some trading cards? Or perhaps
… he hoped … a proper pet. (Not a slug.)

He untied the ribbon. He ripped off the brown paper. He lifted the lid. Then he stared for a full minute.

"Oh," he said.

In the box was an egg, sitting on a nest of crinkly leaves. It was a plain, grey egg. Along the top of the egg was a jagged crack like scribble. Reggie pulled a face. "It's just an old egg."

"And it's broken," sniffed the queen.

"Perhaps we could eat it," said the king.

At that very moment, the egg gave
a little shudder...

CR-AAACK!

"Run!" cried the king.
"It's about to explode."

Chapter 2

Flicker

However, the egg wasn't about to explode at all. It was hatching. The crack grew bigger, and bigger, and BIGGER.

A tiny green foot appeared. Then another. A scaly green head popped up.

"Ooooh!" said Reggie. "It's a tiny dragon!"

The dragon was no bigger than Reggie's right shoe. (Or even his left one.) It was a girl dragon. She had blinking eyes and a flicking orange tongue.

"I shall call you Flicker," Reggie said, tickling the dragon's tail. The little dragon seemed to like this. She let out a puff of red smoke and licked Reggie's hand.

Reggie popped Flicker in the garden among the queen's cabbages. "Don't move," he said sternly. "I'll be right back."

Reggie took out his Tower Power Building Set. He used wood and glue to build a house just the right size for a small dragon. In the downstairs part, he put a thick bed of hay.

When Reggie returned to the garden, he found Flicker snoozing under a cabbage leaf.

Flicker's belly was the size of an orange.

"Look at your belly! What have you been eating?" asked Reggie.

Flicker winked one eye, as if to say, "Something yummy."

Reggie plopped Flicker on her straw bed. "You will make a very good pet," he said and tickled her tail. Flicker let out a rosy puff of breath and licked Reggie's hand.

"Whoa!" cried Reggie, holding his nose. "What a stinker!" Flicker's breath smelt like old pirate boots.

Chapter 3

Sir Plants-a-Lot

The next morning, Reggie woke to the sound of a clink. Then a clunk. Then a very loud CLONK! Flicker had broken one of the walls of her house.

The queen came barging through Reggie's bedroom door, wearing her gardening apron. "Some of the royal cabbages have been eaten," she said in a cross voice.

She waved an empty spray can at Reggie. "And I spent all yesterday afternoon spraying them with Maxi-Gro."

"Maxi-what?" asked Reggie.

"Maxi-Gro," said the queen. "It makes cabbages grow nice and big."

Reggie sniffed. The queen smelt a bit stinky. Or was it the Maxi-Gro? It had an awful smell like … old pirate boots.

Uh-oh! It was the same smell as Flicker's breath. Flicker must have eaten some of the queen's cabbages … and quite a bit of Maxi-Gro too by the smell of it.

The queen went downstairs, and just then, Reggie heard another crash. The top floor of Flicker's house had broken and her wings were sticking through the roof. Wisps of red smoke curled from her snout.

Reggie stared at Flicker, goggle-eyed. She had grown to the size of a cat. "Oh no!" said Reggie. "It must be the Maxi-Gro making you grow, Flicker!"

Reggie plopped Flicker on his bed. "Stay there, and please don't get any bigger," he said. "I'm going to look for help."

Reggie searched the Royal Library for books on gardening. Maybe there was a cure for Maxi-Gro. There *had* to be.

But there didn't seem to be any gardening books in the library. Reggie's heart beat fast when he found a book called *Carrot Tops*. That sounded good. But no, it was about orange jumpers.

Shoots and Leaves was not a gardening book either. It was about a naughty boy who fired arrows at his neighbour and then ran away.

Reggie spied a book called *Dragon Poo for You*.

"Dragon poo?" he muttered. "Yuck!"

He was about to give up when a scrap of paper floated out. It read:

> **Maxi-Gro**
> for super vegetables.
> Invented by
> Sir Plants-a-Lot
> (champion gardener).

"Wow!" cried Reggie. Sir Plants-a-Lot lived in a castle not very far away. "Maybe Sir Plants-a-Lot can cure Flicker."

Reggie hurried to Sir Plants-a-Lot's castle. Beanstalks with fat green pods were growing up the castle walls.

The gatekeeper led Reggie to the garden shed. Sir Plants-a-Lot greeted Reggie with bright, smiley eyes. He held something that looked like a green melon.

"This is my latest invention," said Sir Plants-a-Lot. "This giant pea will feed a family of four." He thrust it under Reggie's nose. "Try some."

Reggie shook his head. He didn't like peas. He explained his dragon problem.

Sir Plants-a-Lot whistled. "You'll need a quick cure. Maxi-Gro is even stronger on dragons than it is on plants."

He glanced at his shelf. "You're in luck. There's a tiny bit of Mini Mix left. I used most of it to shrink a giant beetroot that was taking over my garden."

He handed a bottle to Reggie. "Take care," he warned. "This is the last drop, and I've lost the recipe."

Reggie hugged the bottle tightly and rushed back to the castle.

Chapter 4

Where's Flicker?

Back at Reggie's castle, everyone was getting ready for the Royal Fair. Flags flew from red and blue tents. Streamers hung from the walls.

The queen had set up a long row of tables to display her cabbages. She was planning to put them in a nest of straw. People would be coming from all around to buy the queen's delicious cabbages.

Usually, the money the queen made from selling cabbages was enough to pay the castle bills, and buy food for the whole winter.

Reggie had no time to think about cabbages. He had to feed the Mini Mix to Flicker before she grew any bigger.

He ran up the stairs to his bedroom. Flicker was not on the bed, or in her dragon house. She was nowhere to be seen.

Reggie dashed outside.

"Flicker!" he called urgently and peered into the trees.

A nearby workman paused. "Would Flicker happen to be a dragon?" he asked. Reggie nodded. "With a taste for cabbages?"

Reggie froze. "You don't mean–?"

The workman nodded.

Flicker was in the cabbages again!

Reggie stood in the middle of the queen's vegetable patch. He couldn't believe his eyes. Flicker was bigger than ever.

Her wings flapped in the wind, and her green scales rattled. Her teeth were the size of knives, and right now they were busy munching the last of the queen's cabbages.

Well, nearly the last one. The very last cabbage was buried under a big mound of smelly dragon poo.

Reggie tried to speak, but no words would come out.

"Thundering thunderbolts!" came a voice from behind. The queen dashed into the garden. "My cabbages!" she roared.

"Sorry, Mum," Reggie murmured.

"SORRY?" The queen's eyes almost popped out. "We'll starve!"

"Never mind," said the king, who had just arrived. "I've written a new song. I'm sure people will pay–"

The queen gave him a look. "This is the end!" she shrieked. "We'll all be begging in the streets."

Flicker backed away. Her eyes were the size of plates and her knees knocked together as loudly as drums.

"Here, Flicker," called Reggie nervously.

Beyond the castle wall lay the village of Upper Twaddle. One tread of Flicker's mighty foot could squish an entire house. Reggie couldn't bear to think what would happen if Flicker got out.

"Nice dragon," crooned Reggie. He uncorked the bottle of Mini Mix and waved it under Flicker's huge snout.

"Look what I've got for you."

Flicker snorted in disgust, and pulled up an apple tree with a flick of her tail. Then she stepped over the castle wall.
The ground shook as she thumped towards Upper Twaddle.

Chapter 5

Upper Twaddle

The village of Upper Twaddle was in a panic. "There's a monster on the loose," cried the townspeople.

In the market place, stalls were piled high with food. Flicker roared past like a volcano. Flames shot from her snout.

"Look at my bread," cried the woman at the bread stall. "It's been toasted."

"My tomatoes are all roasted," cried another.

"I'll never sell these sausages," moaned a third. "They've been sizzled into coals."

The villagers chased Flicker, waving their fists. "Stop that dragon!" they cried.

"Don't hurt her!" called Reggie. "She's very gentle. She'll lick your hand if you tickle her tail."

No one took any notice.

Reggie followed Flicker into the countryside. It wasn't hard to see where she had been. Road signs were broken in two.

Fences were flattened. There were burned spots on the bushes and giant dragon footsteps across the fields.

"Whoops!" said Reggie.

The footsteps led through the stony gates of the Knight School.

Everyone knew that knights and dragons did not get along … and that's putting it mildly.

At that moment, the young knights were having a lesson on catching dragons.

"Sir Teach-a-Lot, are dragons very big?" asked a young knight, who was much smaller than the others.

Sir Teach-a-Lot chuckled. "The dragons in our kingdom are tiny," he said. "There's a picture of one in the school library. I'll go and ask Sir Read-a-Lot to find it." Off he dashed.

Just then, a giant shadow fell over the yard. The young knights looked up to see a huge, scaly snout and a flicking, orange tongue. A puff of blood-red smoke drifted over their heads.

"It's a r-real live dragon," said a young knight, trembling in his leather trousers. "What a whopper!"

"We must c-catch it," said the smallest knight bravely. "That's what knights do."

The young knights fetched their ponies. "Here, dragon," they called, as they trotted towards Flicker. Flicker's ears pricked up.

The townspeople came over the hill and shouted, "There's that terrible dragon!"

Sir Teach-a-Lot peered out of the library window. When he saw the giant dragon, he gave an urgent blast on his trumpet.

A hundred guards arrived with fierce-looking swords. Flicker blinked her eyes in fear and flew away.

"Flicker! Come back!" called Reggie.

All he could see was a cloud of dust. He clutched the bottle of Mini Mix to his chest and headed towards the mountain. "I must get to Flicker before the guards do," he said to himself. "It's a matter of life and death."

Chapter 6

Hayfields

Reggie stood on top of the mountain.
He could hear the hooves of the knights'
ponies, and the shouts of the townspeople.
He could see the flash of the guards'
swords … but there was no sign of Flicker.

"If I was a scared dragon, where would
I go?" wondered Reggie. "I know, I'd look
for a big comfy bed of hay."

Reggie looked for a farm. He spied some
haystacks with a puff of smoke as red as a
tomato. Reggie trotted down the mountain
towards it.

Reggie found Flicker snoring in a huge hayfield. Her jumbo-sized body shuddered with each breath. Her scales rattled and her wings twitched.

Reggie tippy-toed towards Flicker's huge head and paused. He had a problem. How could he get a giant dragon to take Mini Mix?

First, he had to wake Flicker. He tickled under one (extra-large) dragon nostril with his hanky. Flicker stopped snoring. Reggie held his breath.

Flicker's eyelashes fluttered. Her great mouth yawned. Her orange tongue flicked in and out.

Quick as a flash, Reggie opened the bottle of Mini Mix. Now all he had to do was to sprinkle a drop on her tongue.

Flicker screwed up her eyes. "Aaah…"

"Oh no!" cried Reggie.

"Aaaaaaaaaaaah…" went Flicker. Reggie turned and ran!

"CHOOOOOOOOOOO."

The giant sneeze blew three haystacks over. It sent a bird backwards. A fluffy cloud changed direction.

In the distance Reggie could hear new sounds. Shouts and cries and the thunder of pony hooves. The dragon hunters were coming.

Any minute they would spot Flicker and then ... Reggie didn't like to think about what might happen after that.

He knew he had to act quickly, but what could he do?

Chapter 7

Reggie Saves the Day

Flicker stretched and flicked her long, orange tongue. Reggie's eyes grew wide. *That's it*, he thought. *I've got it!*

Quickly, Reggie emptied the last drop of Mini Mix onto the palm of his hand. Then he reached out and tickled Flicker's tail. The dragon let out a happy puff, just as she always did.

Reggie tickled her again. Flicker's long tongue flicked towards him. Closer and closer. Reggie held out his hand and Flicker gave it a gentle lick.

WHOOOOSH!

Flicker began to shrink. First she was the size of a pony. Then she was the size of a cat. Finally she was the size of a dragon. (The tiny sort.)

The dragon chasers had seen what happened. They clapped and cheered and whistled.

"Well done," said Sir Teach-a-Lot. "You must come to Knight School and give us a lesson in catching dragons."

"Sure," said Reggie. "As soon as the Royal Fair is over."

Then his heart sank like a stone.

He had been so busy chasing Flicker that he had forgotten she had eaten the royal cabbages. The queen had nothing to sell at the Fair. Sighing, Reggie carried Flicker back to the castle.

When he arrived, he saw the strangest sight. A great forest of cabbages was sprouting from the queen's cabbage patch.

"It's a miracle," said the queen.

"It's magical," said the king.

"It's dragon poo," said Reggie, pointing to the giant droppings. "It's made the cabbages grow bigger than houses."

The queen's face was shiny with happiness. "The Royal Fair will be a huge success," she said.

And it was. Coloured flags flew in the breeze. The king sang his new song, and the townspeople happily carried home huge cabbage leaves.

Reggie made loads of money selling bags of magic dragon poo. He paid the bills for the damage Flicker had caused. With the money left over, he bought enough food to last the Royal Family all winter.

After that, the queen brought Flicker cabbage leaves every day. The king sang his funky pop songs (which Flicker didn't mind). Reggie tickled her tail and told her how clever she was. Flicker let out rosy puffs of smoke. (The happy sort.)

Everyone lived happily ever after.

At least until …

Flicker found the queen's tomato patch.

But that's another story.